A New Home

Story by Colin Dann
Text by Mary Risk
Illustrations by The County Studio

buzz books

KT-155-832

The journey from Farthing Wood had been long and dangerous, but the animals had arrived at last at White Deer Park.

The Great White Stag greeted them.

"You are all heroes," he said. "You have made history. You are welcome to live among us."

MEET ALL THESE FRIENDS IN BUZZ BOOKS:

Thomas the Tank Engine
The Animals of Farthing Wood
Biker Mice From Mars
James Bond Junior
Fireman Sam
Joshua Jones
Rupert
Babar

First published in Great Britain 1994 by Buzz Books,
an imprint of Reed Children's Books
Michelin House, 81 Fulham Road, London SW3 6RB
and Auckland, Melbourne, Singapore and Toronto

ISBN 1 85591 389 5

Printed in Italy by Olivotto

"Very welcome indeed," said a female heron, smiling at Whistler.

Weasel also had an admirer. "Hello, gorgeous," said a male weasel.

But Weasel wasn't interested. "Go away, you measly little beast!" she screamed.

The other animals laughed.

But not everyone at White Deer Park was quite so friendly.

"Who do they think they are?" snarled Scarface, the ferocious blue fox. "This is my territory, and I'm not sharing it."

"Certainly not," sniffed Lady Blue, his mate. "Besides, the new animals are so common. Did you see those red foxes? Huh! Nothing like exotic blue foxes."

"We'll have to teach them a lesson," said Scarface.

The next day, Badger was looking for a
new set in the park.

"Hmm, this looks about right," he said.

"What do you think you're doing?" said a
loud voice.

Badger jumped.

"Eh? What's that? Who's there?" he said.

"You're trespassing," Lady Blue told him.
"You must ask my mate before you move in
anywhere. He's the boss round here."

9

Soon Scarface and Lady Blue were bossing
round the rest of the animals, too.

"He's not *our* leader," said Mother Rabbit.

"Scarface can't tell *us* what to do," the
squirrels declared.

"We need some advice," said Badger.

"And protection," added the mice.

"We need our own leader," said Toad.
"Let's go and see Fox."

10

Fox and Vixen were settling comfortably into their new earth.

"Peace at last," sighed Fox. "Our friends are fine on their own. We can relax now..."

"What was that noise?" said Vixen.

"Fox! We want Fox!" shouted voices from the earth's entrance. "Come out, Fox. You're our leader! We need you!"

Everyone started talking at once.

"Fox, we need your help," said Badger.

"Scarface and Lady Blue have warned us off their land," cried Mole.

"I think they want to eat us," said Mrs Vole with a shudder.

"All right, all right," sighed Fox. "I'll go and have a chat with the Great White Stag."

Stag listened sympathetically.

"Perhaps you and your friends should
have some land of your own where you
can live in peace and safety," he suggested.
"And where no other animal will hunt you.
I'll mark out an area of the park. But
I warn you... " he looked at Fox gravely,
"Scarface won't like it."

13

The Great White Stag kept his promise,
and by the time winter approached, the
Farthing Wood animals were settled in their
own section of the park.

The squirrels collected nuts for their winter
store. Adder slithered beneath a stone and
settled down for her long winter sleep.

"It's time I went into hibernation too,"
said Toad, yawning. He hopped into a hole
on the bank of the pond. "See you in the
spring, mateys!"

The snow came early, and suddenly the food supply dwindled.

"We can't eat our friends," said Vixen.

"We'll have to hunt outside Farthing land," said Fox. "But Scarface won't let us."

They were both growing thin and weak.

15

The herons were having better luck.

"These crayfish aren't bad!" said Whistler's new friend, Speedy, cracking one open with her beak. "Of course, I usually prefer fish, but at times like these..."

She talked on and on.

"Ah! Someone eating! Very good," said Badger, passing by.

16

"Hungry, Badger? Try one," said Whistler.
Badger nibbled at a crayfish doubtfully.

"Hmm, rather fishy," he said, "but better
than nothing. Look here, Whistler old chap,
Fox and Vixen are nearly starving. I don't
suppose you could..."

"Take them some crayfish? Of course," said
Whistler. "There's enough for us all."

17

Fox and Vixen ate the crayfish hungrily.

"It was very kind of Whistler, but these crayfish taste horrible!" said Vixen.

"At least it's food," replied Fox.

"I know," Vixen agreed. "Still, what I wouldn't give for a plump little mouse!"

"No chance of that," said Fox. "Look over there. Scarface is making sure that we don't set a foot outside Farthing land."

Vixen trotted over to the blue foxes.

"Please, listen to me," she said gently.
"When Stag gave this land to the Farthing
Wood animals, he didn't mean for us to be
prisoners here. If you don't let us hunt in
the rest of the park, we'll starve."

"So what," sneered Scarface with a shrug.
"Stag may be the official leader in White
Deer Park, but I've got the *real* power, and
don't you forget it."

No one could forget Scarface. He prowled all round the Farthing land, preventing the animals from hunting in the rest of the park. They felt hungry and miserable, but what could they do?

"I want food!" sobbed Weasel.

"Is that you complaining again, Weasel?"
said Mrs Vole, peeking out from beneath
the snow.

"Mother! Come back!" shouted Mr Vole.

He was a moment too late. Scarface had
already pounced.

Weasel watched in horror.

"You've eaten Mrs Vole," she said. "On Farthing land! That's not allowed!"

"Not allowed?" snarled Scarface. "Nobody tells me what's allowed. I do what I like."

Weasel shrank back with fear. Suddenly it occurred to her that if Scarface had eaten Mrs Vole, he might eat her as well!

"S-sorry, Mr Scarface, sir," she said. "I-I didn't mean..."

Scarface picked Weasel up in his teeth and shook her till her bones rattled.

"Let me go!" shrieked Weasel. "Stop it!"

"On one condition," said Scarface. "From now on, you're going to be my spy. You're going to tell me everything the Farthing Wood animals do — especially Fox."

Weasel wriggled free and ran away.

"Don't forget!" shouted Scarface.

Back at Fox's earth, Fox and Badger were making desperate plans.

"We'll have to scavenge," Badger said. "Raid human gardens and dustbins. We'd be outside Scarface's territory so he couldn't object."

"You're right, my friend," said Fox. "It's our only chance. We'll start tonight."

Owl went ahead to scout out the land.

"Good news!" she hooted. "There's a farm with a henhouse!"

"Come on," said Fox, his mouth watering.

He and Vixen hurried after Owl, but at the entrance to the farm they halted.

26

Frenzied cluckings came from the henhouse. A pair of blue foxes jumped out of the window with dead chickens dangling from their mouths.

Suddenly, the farmer ran towards the henhouse. Fox and Vixen heard several loud bangs, and the blue foxes fell over, dead.

The farmer started towards the dead
chickens. But Fox was quicker.

He leapt over the wall, picked up a
chicken and dashed back to safety. Vixen
raced after him, and picked up the second.

From behind a tree, Scarface had seen it all.

"Two cubs dead, and that miserable Fox has stolen my chickens!" he growled. "I'll get even with those Farthing Wood animals if it's the last thing I do!"